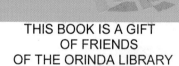

Faraway Farm

For Ella Rose Kennedy and Teddy Traynor
                                              —I.W.

For Holly **—A.A.**

First American edition published in 2006 by Carolrhoda Books, Inc.

Text © 2005 by Ian Whybrow
Illustrations © 2005 by Alex Ayliffe

Originally published in 2005 by Orchard Books, London, England

Carolrhoda Books, Inc.
A division of Lerner Publishing Group
241 First Avenue North
Minneapolis, MN 55401 U.S.A.

Website address: www.lernerbooks.com

Library of Congress Cataloging-in-Publication Data

Whybrow, Ian.
  Faraway Farm / by Ian Whybrow. — 1st American ed.
       p. cm.
  Summary: Simple, rhyming text encourages the reader to search the illustrations for animals and other items found on a farm.
  ISBN-13: 978-1-57505-938-9 (lib. bdg. : alk. paper)
  ISBN-10: 1-57505-938-X (lib. bdg. : alk. paper)
  [1. Farm life—Fiction. 2. Picture puzzles. 3. Stories in rhyme] I. Title.
  PZ8.3.W61926Far 2006
  [E]—dc22   2005026017

Printed and bound in Singapore
1 2 3 4 5 6 – OS -- 11 10 09 08 07 06

Faraway Farm

Ian Whybrow

illustrated by Alex Ayliffe

Carolrhoda Books, Inc. / Minneapolis

Faraway Farm lies over the hill.

Show me the house and the barn and the mill.

Into the kitchen comes Farmer Flat.

Where's his mug and his dog
and his little black cat?

Breakfast!
The children all want to be fed!

Find me some eggs and some milk and some bread.

Time to get ready for milking now.

Where's the stool and the pail and the pretty brown cow?

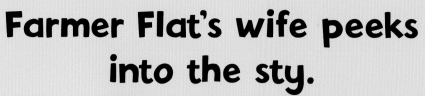

Farmer Flat's wife peeks
into the sty.

She hears an "OINK! OINK!" — so what does she spy?

Here comes the tractor—
the dogs run behind.

What other creatures and birds
can you find?

Over the hill,
where the meadow is steep . . .

show me the rabbit and the
lamb and some sheep.

Here comes the wagon,
all loaded with hay.

Who's in there riding, all done for the day?

Hold out some apples
and quietly stand.

Who'll come and eat them from out of your hand?

Everyone's tired,
so out goes the light.

Who can we find to say,
"Good night! Sleep tight!"

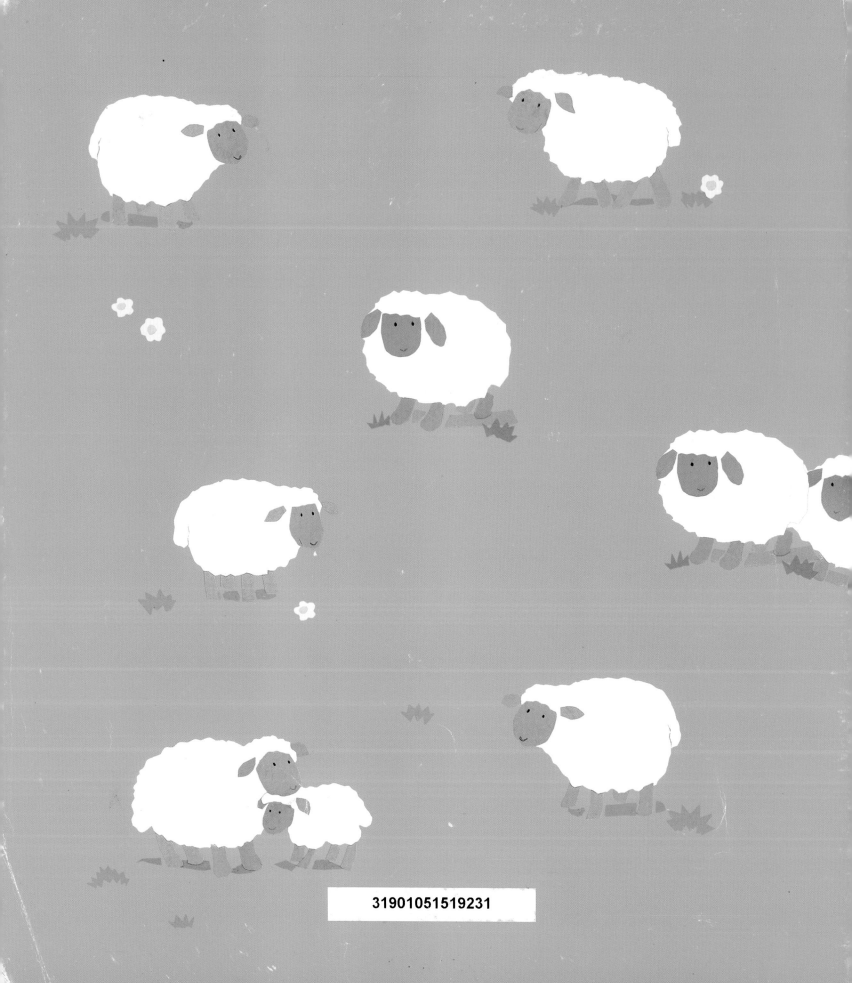